Say Daddy!

Michael Shoulders

Illustrated by Teri Weidner

For Beverly Spiva, a dear friend who
understands one of the most beautiful
words in our language is "book!"

MIKE

For Nicholas Dahlen, with love.

TERI

While speaking in Norfolk, VA, I said, "Parents should begin reading
aloud to their children when they begin talking to them." Since we talk
to our children from the day they are born (sometimes earlier) that is
when we should begin sharing all the gifts found in books.

After my talk, a teacher told me her family began reading to their first child
the day she was born. "She grew to love these things called books," she said.
Her child's first word led me to this story, "Say Daddy!"

—Mike Shoulders

Sleeping Bear Press™

2395 South Huron Parkway, Suite 200
Ann Arbor, MI 48104

Printed and bound in the United States.

10 9 8 7 6 5

Library of Congress Cataloging-in-Publication Data

Shoulders, Michael.
Say Daddy / written by Michael Shoulders; illustrated by Teri Weidner.
p. cm.
Summary: When each family member reads a book to the new baby bear,
they each hope that their name will be the baby's first word, but at a
family celebration everyone is happily surprised.
ISBN 978-1-58536-354-4
[1. Books and reading—Fiction. 2. Animals—Infancy—Fiction.
3. Bears—Fiction.] I. Weidner, Teri. II. Title.

PZ7.S558833Say 2008
[E]—dc22   2007034584

On the day I was born Mother welcomed me into the world
with tears of joy and read me my first book. She said,
"This is a book about life — and how wonderful love is."

She read about kindness, caring, and
how life comes from love.

When Mother closed the last page,
she held me close and whispered,
"Say Mommy! Say Mommy!"
She hoped Mommy would be my first word!

I just stared.

When Daddy brought me home from the hospital,
he read me a book. He said, "This is a book about dreaming—
and how our wishes wrap themselves inside tomorrows
and wait for us. Unfolding them day by day can be fun."

He read about promises and how daddies make dreams come true.

When Daddy closed the last page,
he smiled at me for hours and said,
"Say Daddy! Say Daddy!"
He hoped Daddy would be my first word!

I just made a funny sound.

When my brother played with me for the first time, he read me a book. He said, "This is a book about friendship— and how kindness and fairness shape us and help us grow."

He read about
sand castles on beaches,
bubbles in the wind,

and how brothers are there forever.

When Brother closed the last
page, he rubbed his nose back
and forth on mine, and said,
"Say Bubba! Say Bubba!"
He hoped Bubba would be my first word!

I spit up on him.

When Aunt Grace held me for the first time,
she read me a book. She said, "This is a book about
adventures — and about lands far, far away."

She read about how sometimes important discoveries are not found in distant places, but deep inside our own hearts.

When Aunt Grace closed the last page,
she cuddled me for hours in the bend
of her arm, and said,
"Say Grace! Say Grace!"
She hoped Grace would be my first word!

I just made a funny face.

When Uncle Roy held me for the first time
he read me a book. He said, "This is a book about laughing—
and how, sometimes, it is the best medicine of all."

He read about giggles,
how they spread like waves,

painting smiles on
every face they touch.

When Uncle Roy closed the last page
he tossed me high in the air, laughed
and said, "Say Uncle! Say Uncle!"
He hoped Uncle would be my first word.

I just smelled funny. He gave me back to Mom.

When Grandma rocked me for the first time,
she read me a book. She said, "This is a book about families—
and how they celebrate our joys and hug our tears away."

She read about how families always love, sometimes nearby, sometimes from far, far away, but a family's love is forever.

When Grandma closed the last page,
she rocked me for hours and said,
"Say Nana! Say Nana!"
She hoped Nana would be my first word!

I just goo-gooed.

At our family reunion, everyone brought gifts to the youngest person—ME! Mommy helped me open the first gift, the gold-wrapped one from Grandma. Soon the paper was off.

"BOOK!" I said.
"WHAT did I HEAR?" Daddy asked.
"BOOK!" I said again.
"I HEARD 'BOOK'!" Grandma said.
Everyone stared at me!
I smiled back.

"Say Book!" Mommy said.

"Book!" I said.
Everybody cheered!
Everybody danced!

"NOW, say DADDY!"

Daddy just won't give up!